Lullabies

Also by Lang Leav

Love & Misadventure

Lullabies

Written & Illustrated by
LANG LEAV

Andrews McMeel
Publishing

Kansas City · Sydney · London

Andrews McMeel Publishing, LLC
an Andrews McMeel Universal company
1130 Walnut Street, Kansas City, Missouri 64106

www.andrewsmcmeel.com

14 15 16 17 18 RR2 10 9 8 7 6 5 4 3 2 1

ISBN: 978-1-4494-6107-2

Library of Congress Control Number: 2014941351

The Fell Types are digitally reproduced by Igino Marini.
www.iginomarini.com

ATTENTION: SCHOOLS AND BUSINESSES
Andrews McMeel books are available at quantity discounts
with bulk purchase for educational, business, or sales
promotional use. For information, please e-mail the
Andrews McMeel Publishing Special Sales Department:
specialsales@amuniversal.com.

For Michael

I love you, I do—
you have my word.

You have all
my words.

Contents

INTRODUCTION

"A mind possessed by unmade books."

This line, taken from the poem *Lost Words* by Michael Faudet, illustrates my lifelong preoccupation with books. All artists have a motive, a passion that wills them to create the things they do. For me, it has always been about books. It always will be.

It was from a very young age that I fell in love with this wonderful artifact—the turn of the first page is almost like a sacred ritual to me. Whenever I walk into a library, it is never without some degree of reverence.

Over time, my love of books spilled beyond the joy of reading and I began to dream of books filled with my own words and pictures.

This dream turned to reality with the publication of my first book, *Love & Misadventure*, and continues now with the follow-up, *Lullabies*, the very book you are holding in your hands.

I have always thought poems were a little like spells—incantations that are as old as time. There is a certain quality to words that—when strung in a certain way—has an almost hypnotic effect. This combined with the universal theme of love, becomes ever more potent and intoxicating. After all, what greater magic is there than love?

I hope you enjoy reading *Lullabies* as much as I enjoyed putting it together. I imagine it to be a bedside table kind of book—hopefully, one that you will pick up on some windy, restless night and it will help sing you to sleep.

Though it has a start, middle, and end, you can begin reading *Lullabies* from any page you wish. Some pieces will sing to your present, others may echo of your past, and the rest could whisper of your future. Remember, while the words on these pages remain static, this book—like all other books—is a living and breathing thing. Much like a mirror reflecting its ever-changing landscape, *Lullabies* is a book that, over time, will reveal itself to you slowly.

Much Love,
Lang

Lost Words

A midnight scribble,
    a morning sigh;
    you watch the words
    curl up and die.

Madness lives
    inside your head,
    of poems lost
    and pages dead.

A mind possessed
    by unmade books,
    unwritten lines
    on empty hooks.

—Michael Faudet

Chapter 1

In books unread,
we lie between
their pages.

As they turn us to lovers
like season's changes.

—EXCERPT

Her Words

Love a girl who writes
    and live her many lives;
    you have yet to find her,
    beneath her words of guise.

Kiss her blue-inked fingers,
    forgive the pens they marked.
    The stain of your lips upon her—
    the one she can't discard.

Forget her tattered memories,
    or the pages others took;
    you are her ever after—
    the hero of her book.

My Heart

Perhaps I never loved enough,
    If only I'd loved much more;
    I would not nearly had so much,
    left waiting, for you in store.

If I had given away my heart—
    to those who came before;
    it would be safer left in parts—
    but now you have it all.

Metamorphosis

I am somebody else's story. The girl who served their drink, the person they pushed past on a crowded street, the one who broke their heart. I have happened in so many places, to so many people—the essence of me lives on in these nuances, these moments.

Yet never have I been bolder or brighter than I am with you. Not once have I ever felt so alive. Whatever vessel we pour ourselves into, mine is now overflowing, brimming with life. It is transcending into something new.

Hands are no longer hands. They are caresses. Mouths are no longer mouths. They are kisses. My name is no longer a name, it is a call. And love is no longer love—love is you.

WHEN

When every dream
 has turned to dust,
 and your highest hopes
 no longer soar.

When places you
 once yearned to see,
 grow further away
 on distant shores.

When every night
 you close your eyes,
 and long inside
 for something more.

Remember this
 and only this,
 if nothing else
 you can recall—

There was a life
 a girl once led,
 where you were loved
 the most of all.

Tsunamis

Be careful about giving your heart too quickly, I was told.
Boys only have one thing on their minds, they cautioned.

I don't know if he truly loves me—how can I be sure? I can't say with any conviction that he won't break my heart—but how could I have stopped him from taking what was already his?

He swept in like a tsunami, wave after wave, and I didn't stand a chance. All those warnings, all the things they tried to prepare me for—lost in an instant—to the enormity of what I felt.

Thoughts of You

There were times when I was with him and it was too much. Does that make sense? When someone stirs a world of emotion in you and it's so intense you can barely stand to be with him.

During those moments, I wanted so desperately to leave—to go home, walk into my bedroom, and shut the door behind me. Crawl into bed and lay there in the dark, tracing the outline of my lips with my fingers—replaying everything he said, everything we did. I wanted to be left alone—with nothing other than my thoughts of him.

He's Leaving

My nine
   is your noon;

      I'm just packing now—

your winter,
   my June.

      wish I could pack you.

Patience

Patience and Love agreed to meet at a set time and place; beneath the twenty-third tree in the olive orchard. Patience arrived promptly and waited. She checked her watch every so often but still, there was no sign of Love.

Was it the twenty-third tree or the fifty-sixth? She wondered and decided to check, just in case. As she made her way over to the fifty-sixth tree, Love arrived at twenty-three, where Patience was noticeably absent.

Love waited and waited before deciding he must have the wrong tree and perhaps it was another where they were supposed to meet.

Meanwhile, Patience had arrived at the fifty-sixth tree, where Love was still nowhere to be seen.

Both begin to drift aimlessly around the olive orchard, almost meeting but never do.

Finally, Patience, who was feeling lost and resigned, found herself beneath the same tree where she began. She stood there for barely a minute when there was a tap on her shoulder.

It was Love.

. . . .

"Where are you?" She asked. "I have been searching all my life." "Stop looking for me," Love replied, "and I will find you."

Passing Time

I feel the end is drawing near,
    would time be so kind to slow?
    You are everything to me, my dear,
    you are all I really know.

But as I sit and wait and fear
    and watch the hours go—

Everything that happened here
    happened long ago.

No Other

There is someone I keep in my heart—I love him and no one else. It is a love that will only die with me.

You may ask, *death could be some time away—what if from now to then, you love someone new?*

Well I can tell you, there is only one love. If any person claims to have loved twice in all their life—they have not loved at all.

WELL WISHES

My love, are you well,
　　past the sea and the swell,
　　out in the world, where danger is fraught.

Amidst the doom and the gloom,
　　and the hospital rooms,
　　where hearts can be bartered and bought.

There are words to betray
　　and the things that we say,
　　can sometimes be snappy and short.

Where the strangers we meet,
　　take us down one way streets,
　　and forgetting is something we're taught.

Where earthquakes will reign,
　　between terror and planes—
　　and colds are so easily caught.

SAD THINGS

Why do you write sad things? he asked. *When I am here, when I love you.*

Because someday, in one way or another, you will be taken from me or I you. It is inevitable. But please understand; from the moment I met you, I stopped writing for the past. I no longer write for the present. When I write sad things, I am writing for the future.

A Pilgrimage

Always seeking,
    each moment fleeting;
    this is where
    my soul will rest.

With you I've fulfilled,
    our destined meeting;
    my tired hand,
    against your chest.

This is the heart,
    that keeps mine beating—
    these are the eyes
    that mine know best.

Loving You

I saw him the other day. His arms around another girl, his eyes when met with mine—were slow in their recognition.

I wonder if he remembers what I once told him.

I will love you forever.

He had smiled at me sadly before giving his reply.

But I am so afraid you may one day stop.

Now all these years later, I am the one who is afraid. Because I love him, I still do. I haven't stopped. I don't think I can. I don't think I ever will.

And/Or

I once wrote a book and called it *And/Or*. It was about choosing between either, or having the option of both.

I'm not sure why I wrote it. Perhaps it had something to do with how I looked at life. My lack of care. My indecision. I wanted everything because I didn't want anything enough.

Then I met you and it changed me. For once in my life, there was something I wanted. So much.

For me, that was the death of the word, *or;* because now, there is no other. It was the end of the word, *and;* for I love only you.

Devotion

He is more to me
    than I.

I love him more
    than I can bear.

So much at times
    I wish to die,
    so I can end this
    on a high.

His Kiss

He has me at his every whim;
    everything starts with him.

To all the boys I used to kiss—
    everything stops with his.

Us

I love him and he loves me.

We spend every moment together. When sleep parts us, we often meet in our dreams.

I like to take naps throughout the day. *Like a cat*, he says. He is a cat person.

He thinks my eyes are beautiful and strange. He has never seen eyes like mine up close before.

He says they look at him with daggers when he has done something wrong. Like when he forgets to order olives on my half of the pizza.

He thinks I am especially cute when angry.

We argue over whose turn it is to put the DVD in the player. Sometimes no one wins and we end up watching bad TV. Which is never really a bad thing.

He never imagined he would be with someone like me.

Now, he says, he can't imagine himself with anyone else.

. . . .

We're kids, aren't we?
Yes, kids with grown-up powers.

Signposts

What if certain people were signposts in your life? Representations of good or bad. Like an old friend you see across a crowded street, one you wave hello to, before hurrying on. The last time you saw them, things took a turn for the worse and, as sad as it may seem, they have unwittingly become an omen—a precursor of bad luck.

Or that one person whom you rarely speak with, who can always be found right where you left them. You carry their smile with you like a talisman—for whatever reason, their presence in your life will always bring the promise of better days.

Then there is the boy you can never stop thinking about. Whenever you see his name, it trips you up. Even if it's one that belongs to many others, even if he belongs to someone else.

You know he is a symbol of your weakness, your Kryptonite. How he rushes in like wildfire and burns through everything you worked so hard to build since he last left you in ashes.

So you do the only thing you know how—you put as many miles as you can between him. As many roadblocks and traffic lights as you can gather. Then you build a bold red stop sign right on your doorstep, knowing all the stop signs in the world could never hold him—they can only ask him to stay awhile.

Mementos

You were none,
    and now you're all;
    your worth will rise,
    the more I fall.

Like these mementos
    we have stored,
    once were things—
    now so much more.

Keys

Hearts don't have locks, she said.

Some do, he replies. There are people who give away the key to theirs for safekeeping. Others are mistrustful and give out several keys, just in case. Then there are those who have misplaced them but never cared to look.

What about your heart, she asked.

He smiled.

Your words are the key to mine, he replied.

Never forget your words.

Déjà Vu

I saw it once,
    I have no doubt;
    but now can't place
    its whereabouts.

I try to think it,
    time and time;
    but what it is,
    won't come to mind.

A word, a scent—
    a feeling, past.
    It will not show,
    though much I've asked.

And when it comes,
    I soon forget—
    this is how it felt,
    when we first met.

Clocks

Here in time,
    you are mine;
    my heart has not
    sung louder.

I do not know
    why I love you so—
    the clock knows not
    its hour.

Yet it is clear,
    to all that's here,
    that time is told
    by seeing.

Even though
    clocks do not know,
    it is the reason
    for their being.

Lullabies

I barely know you, she says, voice heavy with sleep. I don't know your favorite color or how you like your coffee. What keeps you up at night or the lullabies that sing you to sleep. I don't know a thing about the first girl you loved, why you stopped loving her or why you still do.

I don't know how many millions of cells you are made of and if they have any idea they are part of something so beautiful and unimaginably perfect.

I may not have a clue about any of these things, but this—she places her hand on his chest—*this* I know.

Message in a Bottle

No one truly knows who they are, he sighs. The glass bottle does not know its own contents. It has no idea whether it is a vessel for the most delicious apple cider, a lovingly crafted wine, or a bitter poison. People are the same. Yet like the bottle, we are transparent. We can't see ourselves the way others see us.

How do you see me? she asked.

You are a bottle floating out at sea, he says. One that contains a very important message. It may never reach its recipient, but as long as there is someone waiting, it will always have purpose.

Will you wait for mine?

I will, he promised. I will look for you every time I stand at the edge of the ocean.

You

There are people I will never know
    and their lives will still ensue;
    those that could have loved me so
    and I'll never wonder who.

Of all the things to come and go,
    there is no one else like you.

The things I never think about—
    and the only thing I do.

More than Love

Love was cruel,
    as I stood proud;
    he showed me you
    and I was bowed.

He deftly dealt
    his swiftest blow—
    I fell further than,
    I was meant to go.

And he ashamed,
    of what he'd caused,
    knew from then,
    that I was yours.

That he, an echo
    and you, the sound—
    I loved you more
    than love allowed.

Second Chances

The path from you extending,
    I could not see its course—
    or the closer to you I was getting,
    the further from you I'd walked.

For I was moving in a circle,
    not a line as I had thought—
    the steps I took away from you,
    were taking me towards.

A Phone Call

We said hello at half past one,
    all our chores for the morning done;
    and as we spoke about our day,
    the world began to fall away.

To our highest hopes and deepest fears,
    if I had one wish, I'd wish you here,
    the tantrums and the horror shows,
    the stories only you would know.

All the while with the ticking clock,
    laughing as if we'd never stop;
    we said good night at half past ten—
    at midnight we said good night again.

ENTWINED

There is a line
    I'm yet to sever —
    it goes from me
    to you.

There was a time
    you swore forever,
    and I am captive
    to its pull.

If you were kind,
    you'd cut the tether—
    but I must ask you
    to be cruel.

STAY

The words I heard
    from you today,
    are said when
    there's nothing
    left to say.

What I would give
    to make you stay,

I would give it
    all away.

The Seventh Sea

The answer is yes, always yes. I cannot deny you anything you ask. I will not let you bear the agony of not knowing.

Yes I love you, I swear it. On every grain of salt in the ocean—on all my tears. I found you when I reached the seventh sea, just as I had stopped looking.

It seems a lifetime ago that I began searching for you.

A lifetime of pain and sorrow. Of disappointment and missed opportunities.

All I had hoped for. All the things I can never get back.

When I am with you, I want for nothing.

Over My Head

I count his breaths,
   in hours unslept,
   against hours of him,
   I have left.

With him lying there,
   with him unaware,
   I am out of my depth.

If My Life Were a Day

You are the moment before the sun sinks into the horizon. The transient light—the ephemeral hues set against the fading, fading sky.

Until I am left only with the moon to refract your light. And in your absence, the stars to guide me—like a cosmic runway—steadily into the dark.

*She was different from anything
he had ever known.*

——THE PROFESSOR

Chapter 2

Interlude

Nostalgia

Do you remember our first day? The fog lifted and all around us were trees linking hands, like children playing.

Our first night, when you stood by the door, conflicted, as I sat there with my knees tucked under my chin, and smiling.

Then rainbows arching over and the most beautiful sunsets I have ever seen.

How the wind howls as the sea whispers, *I miss you.*

Come back to me.

The Professor

A streak of light flashes across the sky. Thick heavy raindrops pound the uneven dirt floor, littered with dried leaves and twigs. She follows closely behind him, clutching an odd contraption—a rectangular device attached with a long, squiggly, antenna. "You were right about the storm, Professor!" she yells over the howling wind. "Yes, my assistant!" he cries, voice charged with excitement, as he holds up the long, metal conductor. She stumbles over a log as he reaches out to catch her.

They tumble on the dry grass laughing. He tosses aside the bent, silver coat hanger, wrapping his arms around her waist. The little transistor radio falls from her hands.

The sun peeks through the treetops.

She thinks of their first conversation. "I live by a forest," he said, describing it in such a way that when she came to scale those crooked, winding stairs, it was like she had seen it a thousand times before. As if it had always been there, waiting to welcome her. Like the pretty, sunlit room that remained unfurnished, sitting empty in his house, now filled with her paints and brushes.

She would fondly call him her Frankenstein, this man who was a patchwork of all the things she had ever longed for. He gave her such gifts—not the kind that were put in boxes, but the sort that filled her with imagination, breathing indescribable happiness into her life. One day, he built her a greenhouse. "So you can create your little monstrous plants," he explained.

He showed her how to catch the stray butterflies that fluttered from their elusive neighbors, who were rumored to farm them for cosmetic use. She would listen in morbid fascination as he described how the helpless insects were cruelly dismembered, before their fragile wings were crushed and ground into a fine powder. "Your lips would look beautiful, painted with butterfly wings," he would tease her.

"Never!" she'd cry, alarmed.

They spent much of their days alone, in their peaceful sanctuary, apart from the little visitor who came on weekends. When the weather was good, the three of them would venture out, past the worn jetty and picnic on their little beach. He would watch them proudly, marveling at the startling contrast between the two things he loved most in the world. His son with hair of spun gold, playing at his favorite rock pool and chattering animatedly in his singsong voice. She, with a small, amused smile on her tiny lips, raven hair tousled by the sea wind. She was different from anything he had ever known.

The Dinner Guest

The wine, sipped too quickly, has gone to my head. I watch the way your hands move as you tell your joke and laugh a little too loudly when you deliver the punch line.

His eyes flash at me from across the table. The same disapproving look he shot me earlier, as I was getting dressed.

It's a bit tight.

Don't be ridiculous, I say.

How do you know him, again?

Just an old friend. We worked together years ago.

He clears his throat, breaking my reverie. My grin fades into a small, restrained smile.

You top up his glass.

The conversation drifts into stocks and bonds. My mind begins to wander, like a bored schoolgirl.

Your hand brushes my leg.

Was it an accident? I look at you questioningly, but you are staring straight ahead, engrossed in conversation.

Then there it is again. Very deliberately, resting on my knee.

Oh, your hands.

They slide up my thigh and under my skirt, lightly skimming the fabric of my panties.

It's been so long.

I part my legs under the table.

The conversation turns to politics.

A mirror effect, you say.

He looks confused. What's this about mirrors?

The word sends a jolt through my body.

Your hand slips into my panties.

Vania

Vania Zouravliov, *that's* his name! My favorite artist. I wanted his book that time . . . very badly, in fact. I tipped my little coin purse upside down and counted all my money. I was short twenty dollars!

She lies on her stomach by the fire with her sketchpad open, lazy pencil strokes lining the paper with each flick of her wrist.

Oh, poor you, he says sympathetically. Do you know what, sweetheart, we'll get you that book.

Thanks, baby. She smiles at him then returns to her sketching.

I'll tell you how, he continues, snapping his laptop shut.

She looks up, bemused. Pencil down, chin propped in hand. *I'm list-en-ing,* she says in a singsong voice.

Okay, so here's what you do. You go into the bookstore and you buy a cheap paperback novel. Smile sweetly and make small talk with the people at the register. Turn on the charm, *just* like the way you do when you're trying to flog me your sketches. "Hey look! I just drew these. What do you think? D'you wanna buy them?"

She giggles.

Then, he says, after you've finished paying, wander over to where the book is, pick it up and flip through it, looking as if you didn't have a care in the world.

He lets out a small chuckle, leaning forward.

Then my dear, you get as close as you can to the entrance without attracting any attention. *And... you bolt!* As fast as you can, down the escape route that we would have planned the day before. I'll be in the car waiting so as soon as you jump in, I'll put my foot down, *hard,* on the accelerator, speed off to somewhere quiet before we stop and I'll look at you and say, Can you believe you did that? How does it feel? And you'll be sitting there, your adrenaline pumping, your heart racing, hugging the book against your chest, saying, "Oh my God! I *can't* believe I just did that!" Then do you know what I'd do?

What—would—you—do? she says between peals of laughter.

I'd take you out, *fuck* you up against the car.

Dumplings

Her impatient hands work slowly.

Like this, she says.

Then you dip your finger in the egg yolk.

Put it between the sheet and press it down firmly.

She watches as he fumbles.

The little pocket of pastry is foreign in his hands.

She reaches out, placing hers on either side of his face. Pulling him towards her, she kisses him warmly.

This is why I love you.

The sides of his face are white from her flour-coated hands.

It makes her laugh.

If only you could see yourself the way I do.

He smiles sheepishly.

Yours are so pretty, he says.

He puts down the oddly shaped dumpling.

And picks up another sheet of pastry.

The Garden

The curtain, a smoky gray color, drops from the creamy white ceiling. Crawling with strange bugs and eight-legged creatures, from where an ominous fan whirs.

His hand reaches for the cord. A string of shiny, black beads that glisten against the bright, early evening sun.

Flashback to the time he found her in the garden. White cotton dress pulled up around her thighs, feet blackened by the rich, lush earth that she had just been turning. With an apologetic smile that said, I couldn't help myself.

THAT NIGHT

It was one of those nights that you are not altogether sure really did happen. There are no photographs, no receipts, no scrawled journal entries.

Just the memory sitting in my mind, like a half-blown dandelion, waiting to be fractured, dismembered. Waiting to disintegrate into nothing.

As I close my eyes, the pictures play like a blurry montage. I can see us driving for hours, until the street signs grew less familiar— the flickering lamplights giving away to stars. Then sitting across from you in that quiet, little Italian place. Your hands pushing the plates aside, reaching across for mine.

The conversations we had about everything and nothing. And kissing you. How I remember that.

It was one of those nights that my mind still can't be sure of. That wonders if I was ever there at all. Yet in my heart, it is as though I've never left.

They gave us years,
though many ago;
the spring cries tears—
the winter, snow.

——MELANCHOLY SKIES

Chapter 3

Finale

THREE QUESTIONS

What was it like to love him? asked Gratitude.
It was like being exhumed, I answered. And brought to life in a flash of brilliance.

What was it like to be loved in return? asked Joy.
It was like being seen after a perpetual darkness, I replied. To be heard after a lifetime of silence.

What was it like to lose him? asked Sorrow.
There was a long pause before I responded:

It was like hearing every good-bye ever said to me—said all at once.

ACCEPTANCE

There are things I miss
    that I shouldn't,
    and those I don't
    that I should.

Sometimes we want
    what we couldn't—
    sometimes we love
    who we could.

FADING POLAROID

My eyes were the first to forget. The face I once cradled between my hands, now a blur. And your voice is slowly drifting from my memory, like a fading polaroid. But the way I felt is still crystal clear. Like it was yesterday.

There are philosophers who claim the past, present, and future all exist at the one time. And the way I have felt, the way I feel—that bittersweet ache between wanting and having—is evidence of their theory.

I felt you before I knew you and I still feel you now. And in that brief moment between—wrapped in your arms thinking, *how lucky I am, how lucky I am, how lucky I am*—

How lucky I was.

Thoughts

Dawn turns to day,
    as stars are dispersed;
    wherever I lay,
    I think of you first.

The sun has arisen,
    the sky, a sad blue.
    I quietly listen—
    the wind sings of you.

The thoughts we each keep,
    that are closest to heart,
    we think as we sleep—
    and you're always my last.

Dyslexia

There were letters I wrote you that I gave up sending, long before I stopped writing. I don't remember their contents, but I can recall with absolute clarity, your name scrawled across the pages. I could never quite contain you to those messy sheets of blue ink. I could not stop you from overtaking everything else.

I wrote your name over and over—on scraps of paper, in books and on the back of my wrists. I carved it like sacred markings into trees and the tops of my thighs. Years went by and the scars have vanished, but the sting has not left me. Sometimes when I read a book, parts will lift from the pages in an anagram of your name. Like a code to remind me it's not over. Like dyslexia in reverse.

Dead Poets

Her poetry is written on the ghost of trees, whispered on the lips of lovers.

As a little girl, she would drift in and out of libraries filled with dead poets and their musky scent. She held them in her hands and breathed them in—wanting so much to be part of their world.

It wasn't long before Emily began speaking to her, then Sylvia and Katherine; their voices rang in unison, haunting and beautiful. They told her one day her poetry would be written on the ghost of trees and whispered on the lips of lovers.

But it would come at a price.

There isn't a thing I would not gladly give, she thought, to join my idols on those dusty shelves. To be immortal.

As if reading her mind, the voices of the dead poets cried out in alarm and warned her about the greatest heartache of all—how every stroke of pen thereafter would open the same wound over and over again.

What is the cause of such great heartache? She asked. They heard the keen anticipation in her voice and were sorry for her.

The greatest heartache comes from loving another soul, they said, beyond reason, beyond doubt, with no hope of salvation.

It was on her sixteenth birthday that she first fell in love. With a boy who brought her red roses and white lies. When he broke her heart, she cried for days.

Then hopeful, she sat with a pen in her hand, poised over the blank white sheet, but it refused to draw blood.

Many birthdays came and went.

One by one, she loved them and just as easily, they were lost to her. Somewhere amidst the carnations and forget-me-nots, between the lilacs and mistletoe—she slowly learned about love. Little by little, her heart bloomed into a bouquet of hope and ecstasy, of tenderness and betrayal.

Then she met you, and you brought her dandelions each day, so she would never want for wishes. She looked deep into your eyes and saw the very best of herself reflected back.

And she loved you, beyond reason, beyond doubt, and with no hope of salvation.

When she felt your love slipping away from her, she knelt at the altar, before all the great poets—and she begged. She no longer cared for poetry or immortality, she only wanted you.

But all the dead poets could do was look on, helpless and resigned while everything she had ever wished for came true in the cruelest possible way.

She learned too late that poets are among the damned, cursed to commiserate over their loss, to reach with outstretched hands— hands that will never know the weight of what they seek.

Time

You were the one
    I wanted most
    to stay.

But time could not
    be kept at bay.

The more it goes,
    the more it's gone—
    the more it takes away.

Broken Hearts

I know you've lost someone and it hurts. You may have lost them suddenly, unexpectedly. Or perhaps you began losing pieces of them until one day, there was nothing left. You may have known them all your life or you may have barely known them at all. Either way, it is irrelevant—you cannot control the depth of a wound another inflicts upon you.

Which is why I am not here to tell you tomorrow will be a new day. That the sun will go on shining. Or there are plenty of fish in the sea. What I will tell you is this; it's okay to be hurting as much as you are. What you are feeling is not only completely valid but necessary—because it makes you so much more human. And though I can't promise it will get better any time soon, I can tell you that it will—eventually. For now, all you can do is take your time. Take all the time you need.

Wounded

A bruise is tender
    but does not last,
    it leaves me as
    I always was.

But a wound I take
    much more to heart,
    for a scar will always
    leave its mark.

And if you should ask
    which one you are,
    my answer is—
    you are a scar.

Despondency

There was a girl named Despondency, who loved a boy named Altruistic, and he loved her in return.

She adored books and he could not read, so they spent most of their time wandering through worlds together and in doing so, lived many lives.

One day, they read the last book there was and decided they would write their own. It was a beautiful tale set against a harsh desert with a prince named Mirage as the hero. From their wild imaginings, an intricate plot of adventure and tragedy unfolded.

Altruistic awoke one night to find Despondency sitting at her desk, furiously scribbling away in their book. It caught him by surprise for until now, she had not written a single word without him.

Despondency turned to face him, her eyes cast downward. She told him while writing their story, she had fallen desperately in love with Prince Mirage and wanted to wander the desert in search of him.

Altruistic was heartbroken but knew it was in Despondency's nature to long for what she couldn't have, just like it was in his not to stand in her way. Crying, she begged him to burn the tale of Prince Mirage, but he could not bring himself to do it.

They said their good-byes and she asked him if he would carry their book with him always. He promised he would and with one final look, she was swallowed by the swirling desert sands. He knew he would never see her again.

EPILOGUE

The girl was standing in the graveyard by her father's tombstone when a tall stranger approached. Handing her a worn, leather-bound book, he said, "Your father wanted you to have this." She knew at once it was the book he had carried in his breast pocket, close to his heart for all his life. Her father's inability to read was also something she had inherited, and while tracing her fingers over the cover of the book, she asked, "Can you please tell me what the title is?"

"Grief." the stranger replied.

For You

Here are the things I want for you.

I want you to be happy. I want someone else to know the warmth of your smile, to feel the way I did when I was in your presence.

I want you to know how happy you once made me and though you really did hurt me, in the end, I was better for it. I don't know if what we had was love, but if it wasn't, I hope never to fall in love. Because of you, I know I am too fragile to bear it.

I want you to remember my lips beneath your fingers and how you told me things you never told another soul. I want you to know that I have kept sacred, everything you had entrusted in me and I always will.

Finally, I want you to know how sorry I am for pushing you away when I had only meant to bring you closer. And if I ever felt like home to you, it was because you were safe with me. I want you to know that most of all.

Always with Me

Your love I once surrendered,
    has never left my mind.

My heart is just as tender,
    as the day I called you mine.

I did not take you with me,
    but you were never left behind.

LOVE'S INCEPTION

I did not know
    that it was love
    until I knew.

There was never
    another to compare
    with you.

But since you left,
    each boy I meet,
    will always have you
    to compete.

Karma

Sorrow tells stories,
    I relay them to wisdom;
    I play them like records
    to those who will listen.

I know to be thankful,
    I was given my time;
    to those who have loved him—
    your heartache is mine.

To the one who will keep him,
    and the hearts he has kept
    your love, when it leaves him—
    his greatest regret.

Fairy Tales

When she was a little girl, she went to the school library asking for books about princesses.
You've read every book we have about princesses.
In the whole library?
Yes.

Years later, she fell in love. She wrote his name on the inside of her pencil case. Hoping he might ask to borrow a pen so she could be found out.

In the yard of a house where she lived, there was a large oak tree carved with the initials of each boy she had ever kissed. She put a cross next to the letters F.P. and noticed with a quiet wonder that he shared the same initials as The Frog Prince.

She loved only him.

Like Rapunzel, she grew her hair longer than anyone she knew and for nearly a whole summer, she slept and slept and slept. She stayed inside until her skin turned a powder white against her blood red lips. Each day was spent living and breathing and longing for twisted paths and murderous wolves.

You're living in a fantasy, her mother said.
You need to wake up, her boyfriend told her.

But all she could think about was the boy who was now just an inscription inside a pencil case and two crooked letters carved into an old oak tree.

And the fairy tale his lips once left on the ashen surface of her skin.

A Letter

It was beautifully worded
    and painfully read;
    the things that were written,
    were those never said.

His lies were my comfort,
    but the truth I was owed—
    I so wanted to know it,
    now I wish not to know.

Unrequited

The sun above;
    a stringless kite,
    her tendril fingers
    reach toward.

Her eyes, like flowers,
    close at night,
    and the moon is sad
    to be ignored.

Concentric Circles

Aging is a euphemism for dying, and the age of a tree can only be counted by its rings, once felled.

Sometimes I feel there are so many rings inside me—and if anyone were to look, they would see I have lived and died many times over, each time shedding my leaves bare with the hope of renewal—the desire to be reborn.

Like concentric circles that spill outwards across the water—I wish I could wear my rings on the surface and feel less ashamed of them. Or better yet, to be completely stripped and baptized—my lines vanishing like a newly pressed garment, a still pond.

Edgar's Gift

Anything and everything,
    the two almost the same—
    everything says, have it all;
    anything, one to claim.

If I say, I'd give you everything,
    we know it can never be,
    but I will give you anything—
    I just hope that thing is me.

Pretext

Our love—a dead star
    to the world it burns brightly—

    But it died long ago.

LIVING A LIE

Thoughts that she
    cannot unthink;
    a life that she
    cannot unlive.

Skipping stones
    to watch them sink;
    she envies how
    they easily.

Sorrow wraps her
    like a scarf;
    waiting for a
    small reprieve—
    falling in and out
    of love.

Soundtracks

He once told me about his love for lyrics. How the words spoke to him like poetry.

I would often wonder about his playlist and the ghosts who lived there. The faces he saw and the voices he heard. The soundtrack to a thousand tragic endings, real or imagined.

The first time I saw him, I noticed how haunted his eyes were. And I was drawn to him, in the way a melody draws a crowd to the dance floor. Pulled by invisible strings.

Now I wonder if I am one of those ghosts—if I am somewhere, drifting between those notes. I hope I am. I hope whenever my song plays, I am there, whispering in his ear.

A Winter Song

She was the song,
    in a chorus——unheard.
    You were the summer
    in her winter of verse.

Yours was the melody
    she wanted to learn;
    it clung to her lips,
    in silence it yearned.

It seems as though now,
    you forgot every word;
    in a field full of flowers,
    she was the first.

There once was a song
    you reminded her of——
    she no longer longs,
    yet she still loves.

Two Fishermen

A girl came upon a fisherman at the water's edge and watched as he cast his net into the wide, open sea. On closer inspection, she noticed how all the knots that usually held a net together were unknotted.

"Why do you throw a knotless net into the water?" she asked.

"I want to catch all fish in the ocean," he replied. "But there are none I wish to keep."

She walked on a little further and came across another fisherman, holding a simple line. She studied him quietly as he reeled his catch in, before returning it to the water. After he repeated this several times, the girl asked him, "Why do you catch them just to throw them back?"

"There is only one fish I want to catch and so, no other holds my interest."

SHIPWRECKS

The wild seas for
    which she longed,
    lay far beyond
    the shore.

The shipwreck that
    her lips had sung,
    meant she never
    left at all.

It wasn't 'til
    the tide had won,
    that she learned
    it could not hurt her.

It was the furthest
    she had gone—
    and she never went
    much further.

An Artist in Love

I drew him in my world;
    I write him in my lines,
    I want to be his girl,
    he was never meant as mine.

I drew him in my world;
    He is always on my mind;
    I draw his every line.
    It hurts when he's unkind.

I drew him in my world;
    I draw him all the time,
    but I don't know where
    to draw the line.

False Hope

I don't know if I want you, he says. But I do know I don't want anyone else to have you.

It wasn't good enough, I knew that. Honestly I did. In my mind it was crystal clear. My heart however, was having a serious case of selective hearing. All it heard was, *I don't want anyone else to have you.* And within that—was a glimmer of hope, a spark of optimism.

A Cautionary Tale

There is a girl who never returns her library books. Don't give her your heart—it is unlikely you will ever see it again.

Afterthought

Thoughts I think of presently,
    will come and go with ease—
    while thoughts of you, from long before,
    have yet to make their leave.

The memory of you and I,
    still finds me here and now;
    tomorrow has arrived and gone—
    yet your voice to me, resounds.

For if my present were an echo of,
    a past I can't forget—

Then these thoughts are just
    an afterthought—
    and I am always in its debt.

GROUNDED

The little birds
    who dream of flight;
    who gaze into
    the starry night.

Their tired wings
    fold down and up;
    they try their best
    but it is not enough.

The Very Thing

I often wonder why we want so much, to give others the very thing that we were denied. The mother working tirelessly to provide her child with an education; the little boy who was bullied in school and is now a Nobel Prize-winning advocate for peace. The author who writes happy endings for the characters in her book.

Forewarned

If a boy ever says, you remind me of someone—don't fall in love with him. You will never be anything more than second best.

Mixed Messages

The questions you had never asked
    were things you were afraid to know;
    everything that has come to pass,
    you've made them all up on your own.

There are many words you never said,
    that others dreamed you someday would;
    each of us for all our days—
    will live our lives misunderstood.

Masquerade

As a writer, there is an inclination to step inside someone else's shoes, to get under their skin and see the world through their eyes. In many such scenarios, I have slipped into these roles with the greatest of ease—then out again with the same dexterity.

That was until I found myself in character, playing the girl who falls in love with you. It was then the line between fantasy and reality were so blurred that I no longer knew who I was.

Yet, there was clearly a point when my role was well and truly over. When I had gone above and beyond the required word count. Where I had exhausted every new angle or approach there was to writing our story.

I know it's over, I really do. I know it has been for quite some time. It's over, yet my heart still feels you. You are a memory to me now, but my mind still thinks of you. What we had was finished long ago—yet the words will not stop flowing.

CHANGE OF HEART

You were faultless
    I was flawed,

I was lesser
    yet you
    gave more.

Now with time,
    I find you
    on my mind—

Perhaps I loved you,
    after all.

Reasons

I wish I knew why he left. What his reasons were. Why he changed his mind.

For all these years, I have turned it over in my head—all the possibilities—yet none of them make any sense.

And then I think, perhaps it was because he never loved me. But that makes the least sense of all.

All There Was

My greatest lesson learnt,
    you were mine until you weren't.

It was you who taught me so,
    the grace in letting go.

The time we had was all—
    there was not a moment more.

Pen Portrait

She doesn't keep time,
    so she stopped wearing watches.

Her promise won't bind,
    so no one holds her to them.

She lives in the past,
    so her present never catches—

Her thoughts do not last,
    so her pen must tattoo them.

Musical Chairs

When the music stood still, I was standing at an empty chair.

I could feel you smiling behind me. (We sense these things while dreaming.)

Your hands were on my shoulders, your kisses against my neck.

Then from somewhere, the music of a piano as she sings to Mozart, no one will ever know me the way you do.

Tell Me

Tell me if you ever cared,
    if a single thought
    for me was spared.

Tell me when you lie in bed,
    do you think of something
    I once said.

Tell me if you hurt at all,
    when someone says
    my name with yours.

It may have been so long ago,
    but I would give
    the world to know.

Beach Ball

Do you know that feeling? When it's like you've lost something but can't remember what it was. It's as though you're trying so desperately to think of a word but it won't come to you. You've said it a thousand times before and it was always there—right where you left it. But now you can't recall it. You try and try to make it appear and it almost does, but it never does.

There are times when I think it could surface—when I sense it at the tip of my tongue. When I feel it struggling to burst from my chest like a beach ball that can only be held beneath the water for so long.

I can feel it stirring each time someone hurts me. When I smile at a stranger and they don't smile back. When I trust someone with a secret and they betray me. When someone I admire tells me I am not good enough.

I don't know what it is or what I have lost. But I know it was important, I know it once made me happy.

Amends

I wonder if there will be a morning when you'll wake up missing me. That some incident in your life would have finally taught you the value of my worth. And you will feel a surge of longing, when you remember how I was good to you.

When this day comes I hope you will look for me. I hope you will look with the kind of conviction I'd always hoped for, but never had from you. Because I want to be found. And I hope it will be you—who finds me.

The Most

You may not know
 the reason why,
 for a time
 I wasn't I.

There was a man
 who came and went,
 on him every breath
 was spent.

I'm sorry I forgot
 all else—
 it was the most
 I ever felt.

History

In the beginning, I wrote to you and you wrote back. For the first time, I had something worth writing about.

Then somewhere during our correspondence, I deviated—and instead of writing to you, I began writing for you. There was so much to say, things I couldn't tell you and I sensed it was important to put them down somewhere. For inherently, mankind is compelled to record their greatest moments in history and you were mine.

I don't write to you anymore. Nor do I write for you. But I do write—and every word still aches for you.

The Dream

I saw a dream
  long lost to me,
  in search of
  another's waking.

It found a shoreline
  far away
  as the day—
  as my heart,
  was breaking.

And I sighed and wept
  for what could not be—
  and for all that could
  have been,

For every hope
  and every prayer
  long drowned
  beneath the sea.

I fell to sleep
  alone that night,
  to the sound
  of a distant call.

The faintest whisper
  of good-bye—
  and the dream
  was mine, no more.

WISHING STARS

I still search
    for you in crowds,
    in empty fields
    and soaring clouds.

In city lights
    and passing cars,
    on winding roads
    and wishing stars.

I wonder where
    you could be now,
    for years I've not said
    your name out loud.

And longer since
    I called you mine—
    time has passed
    for you and I.

Yet I have learned
    to live without,
    I do not mind—
    I still love you anyhow.

Forever for Now

Stretching out from here to then,
    days before us,
    came and went.

Someday we will meet again,
    for now the end—
    of days on end.

Nostalgia for Today

Do you remember what you once said to me?

One day you will be nostalgic for today.

At the time, I couldn't begin to conceive a future without you—I believed with all my heart we were destined for each other. And in the back of my mind, I always knew I'd feel nostalgic for a moment we shared or a memory we created—but not once, not even for a second—did I imagine it was you I would be nostalgic for.

Poker Face

There was a time I would tell you,
   of all that ached inside;
   the things I held so sacred,
   to all the world I'd hide.

But they became your weapons,
   and slowly I have learnt,
   the less that is said, the better—
   the lesser I'll be hurt.

Of all you've used against me,
   the worst has been my words.

There are things I'll never tell you,
   and it is sad to think it so;
   the more you come to know me—
   the less of me you'll know.

CROSSWORDS

I write to bring you closer. To imagine your fingers trailing the curve of my spine. To recall how the span of your hands were exactly the width of my hips. And how our bodies would fall into each other like words on a crossword puzzle. I write for the raw ache in my bones when the ink seeps into paper—for the bittersweet sorrow that comes from bringing you back.

Forget Me Not

The choice was once
    your choosing,
    before losing
    became my loss.
    I was there in
    your forgetting—
    until I was forgot.

Melancholy Skies

Three summers passed
    of sun-drenched dreams,
    of snow white clouds
    and you and me.

The warmth of love,
    all summer long,
    through winter's chill
    we'd carry on.

Each season's end
    began anew,
    until the last—
    I shared with you.

They gave us years,
    though many ago;
    the spring cries tears—
    the winter, snow.

The Poet

Why do you write? he asked.

So I can take my love for you and give it to the world, I reply.

Because you won't take it from me.

Almost

Do you see
    how I love him true—
    it could have been you.

As for you
    and your love for she—
    it could have been me.

But we were a maybe,
    and never a must—
    when it should have been us.

HE'S FORGOTTEN

Time is to wound
     like wound is to suture,
     when she was his past
     and he is her future.

PERFECT

He said to me "You're perfect,
    and I want you to be mine."
    But I felt I wasn't worthy
    and to be perfect, I'll need time.

I knew it would be worth it,
    I could be better if I tried,
    then he got tired of waiting—
    and I watched my chance go by.

Minefield

If you know a boy with eyes of quiet wonderment, who smiles often and speaks rarely—someone who pays the same respect to words as he would a minefield—who thinks deeply and is endearingly sad—please do not give your heart to him. Even when he gently pleads with you—or clutches your hand with grave earnest—no matter how he tries to convince you, please turn him away. You don't know him like I know him. You can't love him like I do.

A Sad Farewell

For all the time I've known you,
    to the present—now our past;
    I know never to forget you;
    though regret still pains my heart.

Had I known, I would not have left you,
    alone beneath those stars,
    on the night when I last saw you,
    not knowing it was the last.

Regrets

Timing is irrelevant when two people are meant for each other. It's what I once believed.

But we met during a time when I was such a mess, when I still had so much to figure out. How could I have known how crucial every word, every action was or how losing you would be something I would always regret?

If only you could have met me now, how different it would be. How much I have changed. How I have grown. I learned so much from all the mistakes I made with you. I just wish I had made them with someone else.

Ode to Sorrow

Her eyes, a closed book,
    her heart, a locked door;
    she writes melancholy
    like she's lived it before.

She once loved in a way,
    you could not understand;
    he left her in pieces
    and a pen in her hand.

The ode to her sorrow
    in the life she has led—
    her scratches on paper,
    the words they have bled.

Remembering You

The day you left, I went through all my old journals, frantically looking for the first mention of you. Searching for any details I can no longer recall—any morsel of information that may have been lost to my subconscious. The memory of you is fading, a little at a time, and I can feel myself forgetting. I don't want to forget.

Love's Paradox

There is a tide that rolls away,
    I want to make it stay.

A borrowed book sits on my shelf,
    I want it for myself.

There are two old hands
      that move this clock,
      I want to make them stop.

There is a love you sold to me,
    I keep it under lock—
      and yet you hold the key.

A Ghost

His voice in this room,
    like shadows on walls;
    I imagine him on
    the other side of the door.

His voice, his hands, his touch,
    at the start, the end,
    and in the middle.

Strange how it mattered so much,
    when now it matters
    so little.

Losing You

I used to think I couldn't go a day without your smile. Without telling you things and hearing your voice back.

Then, that day arrived and it was so damn hard but the next was harder. I knew with a sinking feeling it was going to get worse, and I wasn't going to be okay for a very long time.

Because losing someone isn't an occasion or an event. It doesn't just happen once. It happens over and over again. I lose you every time I pick up your favorite coffee mug; whenever that one song plays on the radio, or when I discover your old t-shirt at the bottom of my laundry pile.

I lose you every time I think of kissing you, holding you, or wanting you. I go to bed at night and lose you, when I wish I could tell you about my day. And in the morning, when I wake and reach for the empty space across the sheets, I begin to lose you all over again.

The End

"I don't know what to say," he said.

"It's okay," she replied, "I know what we are—
and I know what we're not."

Encore

Excerpts from
Love & Misadventure

Also by Lang Leav

*Available where all
good books are sold*

ANGELS

It happens like this. One day you meet someone and for some inexplicable reason, you feel more connected to this stranger than anyone else—closer to them than your closest family. Perhaps because this person carries an angel within them—one sent to you for some higher purpose, to teach you an important lesson or to keep you safe during a perilous time. What you must do is trust in them—even if they come hand in hand with pain or suffering—the reason for their presence will become clear in due time.

Though here is a word of warning—you may grow to love this person but remember they are not yours to keep. Their purpose isn't to save you but to show you how to save yourself. And once this is fulfilled, the halo lifts and the angel leaves their body as the person exits your life. They will be a stranger to you once more.

. . . .

It's so dark right now, I can't see any light around me.
That's because the light is coming from you. You can't see it but everyone else can.

SOULS

When two souls fall in love, there is nothing else but the yearning to be close to the other. The presence that is felt through a hand held, a voice heard, or a smile seen.

Souls do not have calendars or clocks, nor do they understand the notion of time or distance. They only know it feels right to be with one another.

This is the reason why you miss someone so much when they are not there—even if they are only in the very next room. Your soul only feels their absence—it doesn't realize the separation is temporary.

. . . .

Can I ask you something?
Anything.
Why is it every time we say good night, it feels like good-bye?

A Dream

As the Earth began spinning faster and faster, we floated upwards, hands locked tightly together, eyes sad and bewildered. We watched as our faces grew younger and realized the Earth was spinning in reverse, moving us backwards in time.

Then we reached a point where I no longer knew who you were and I was grasping the hands of a stranger. But I didn't let go. And neither did you.

. . . .

I had my first dream about you last night.
Really? She smiles. What was it about?
I don't remember exactly, but the whole time I was dreaming, I knew you were mine.

Rogue Planets

As a kid, I would count backwards from ten and imagine at one, there would be an explosion—perhaps caused by a rogue planet crashing into Earth or some other major catastrophe. When nothing happened, I'd feel relieved and at the same time, a little disappointed.

I think of you at ten; the first time I saw you. Your smile at nine and how it lit up something inside me I had thought long dead. Your lips at eight pressed against mine and at seven, your warm breath in my ear and your hands everywhere. You tell me you love me at six and at five we have our first real fight. At four we have our second and three, our third. At two you tell me you can't go on any longer and then at one, you ask me to stay.

And I am relieved, so relieved—and a little disappointed.

Sea of Strangers

In a sea of strangers,
   you've longed to know me.
   Your life spent sailing
   to my shores.

The arms that yearn
   to someday hold me,
   will ache beneath
   the heavy oars.

Please take your time
   and take it slowly;
   as all you do
   will run its course.

And nothing else
   can take what only—
   was always meant
   as solely yours.

Closure

Like time suspended,
    a wound unmended—
    you and I.

We had no ending,
    no said good-bye.

For all my life,
    I'll wonder why.

Acknowledgments

Thank you to my agent, Al Zuckerman, for his invaluable guidance and wonderful support.

To Kirsty Melville and her passionate team at Andrews McMeel, for sending my books out into the world.

To all the amazing people I have had the pleasure of meeting on my book tours (you know who you are), thank you for working so tirelessly behind the scenes and for making me feel so welcome on my visits.

To my family and friends, it goes without saying that I wouldn't be here without your love and encouragement.

To Ollie Faudet, who likes cows and makes me laugh.

And last, but definitely not least—a very special thank you to all of my beautiful readers. Your unwavering support and kind words inspire me every day.

About the Author

The work of poet and artist Lang Leav swings between the whimsical and woeful, expressing a complexity beneath its childlike facade.

Lang is a recipient of the Qantas Spirit of Youth Award and a prestigious Churchill Fellowship.

Her artwork is exhibited internationally and she was selected to take part in the landmark Playboy Redux show curated by the Andy Warhol Museum.

She currently lives with her partner and collaborator, Michael, in a little house by the sea.

Index

Encore 219

POSTED POEMS

Posted Poems is a unique postal service that allows you to send your favorite Lang Leav poem to anyone, anywhere in the world. All poems are printed on heavyweight art paper and encased in a beautiful string-tie envelope. To send a Posted Poem to someone special visit: langleav.com/postedpoems